BEAUTIFUL JOE

THE TRUE STORY OF A BRAVE DOG

By Marshall Saunders

Retold by Quinn Currie

Illustrated by Susan Heinonen

Storytellers Ink
Seattle, Washington

ISBN 0-962-30721-1

Printed in the United States of America

Published by Storytellers Ink • Seattle, Washington

INTRODUCTION

If there is one all-time North American dog classic, that honor surely belongs to the book *Beautiful Joe*. Although it was written a hundred years ago, it has touched the hearts of millions of readers throughout the world. It will, I believe, in this handsome new edition, now touch a whole new generation.

Beautiful Joe himself, a brown mutt, was not handsome - in fact he was almost called "Ugly Joe." But he was beautiful inside, and he had a beautiful mistress who would never allow him to be called "Ugly." So the boy who rescued him called him "Beautiful."

Beautiful Joe is a true story - about a dog who was born in a stable on the outskirts of a small town in Maine called Fairport. Marshall Saunders, one of Canada's most famous writers, learned the story of the dog from American friends, and she spent six months with Beautiful Joe and the family who adopted him before writing his story.

Ms. Saunders never married, but traveled widely in America and Europe and wrote many other books. "But wherever I went," she wrote, "*Beautiful Joe* kept barking at me."

Throughout her life her passion was kindness to animals. She wrote, as one author friend described her, "not as though she merely desired to write a book, but because her heart burned within her." Another spoke of "the wealth of her creative mind, and her generous soul." Still a third said she had "an infinite capacity for kindliness to dumb creatures - whether they walk, hop, crawl, or slither."

Such qualities were evident in Ms. Saunder's final book about Beautiful Joe. It was called *Beautiful Joe's Paradise*. Long disturbed by people who said that animals did not go to Heaven when they died, Ms. Saunders decided to write a book about Animal Heaven. Ms. Saunders' father told her she should make her "old Favorite," Joe, the hero of her paradise.

But at first Ms. Saunder's refused:

> "Almost shocked at the idea of trading, as it were, on the popularity of the dear old animal, I said frimly, 'I cannot do that. I shall never bring Joe into another story.'"

But when she herself lost one of her own dogs she relented:

> "However, last autumn, when in great grief over the death of a beloved dog my mind turned strongly to my animal story. Old Joe was ever before me. He, and only he, was suited to preside over the happy republic where the animals found themselves after death."

Joe is indeed "President" of the Animals' Heaven, and it is to this Heaven that a boy visits - a boy who has just lost his own dog and has been told that animals do not go to Heaven. Here the boy meets not only dogs and cats but also birds and fish and elephants and lions and tigers and bears and monkeys and all the other animals. All are at peace with each other, because all are vegetarians. And, in charge of them all is Beautiful Joe. But Joe will not remain president of the Animals' Heaven forever because, we are promised, when his mistress dies, Joe will give up his Presidency and return to her side.

Meanwhile, all of us still here on earth can return to the story of Beautiful Joe.

- Cleveland Amory

Contents

1

Just a Mutt

My name is Beautiful Joe, and I am a medium-sized brown dog. I am called Beautiful Joe, but not because I am a beauty. I know that I am not beautiful, and I know that I am not well-bred. My mistress went every year for my license, and when the man in the office asked what breed I was, she would always say part fox-terrier and part bull-terrier; but he always put me down as a mutt. I don't think she liked him calling me a mutt.

I love my mistress more than anyone else in the world. She loves all animals, and it grieves her to see them treated cruelly.

I have heard her say that if all boys and girls in the world were to rise up and say that there should be no more cruelty to animals, they could put a stop to it. The more stories that are written about animals, the better it will be for us. Perhaps it will help a little if I tell my story.

I was born in a stable on the outskirts of a small town in Maine called Fairport. The first thing I remember was lying close to my mother and being very snug and warm. The next thing I remember was always being hungry. I had brothers and sisters - six in all - and my mother never had enough milk for us. She was half-starved herself, so was unable to feed us properly.

It is hard for me to talk about my early life because I have lived so long now in a wonderful family where there is never a harsh word spoken, and where no one would think of ill-treating anybody or anything.

The man who owned my mother was an ice delivery man. He kept one horse and two cows, and had a shaky old cart in which he used to put his ice. There can't be a worse man in the world than that ice man. It makes me shudder to think of him.

His name was Jenkins, and the first notice he took of me, when I was a little puppy just able to stagger about, was to give me a kick that sent me across the floor. He used to beat and starve my mother. I have seen him use his heavy whip to punish her till her body was covered with blood.

Another problem of Jenkins' was his laziness. After he did his rounds in the morning, he had nothing to do till late in the afternoon but take care of his stable and yard. If he had kept them neat, and groomed his horse, and cleaned the cows, and cultivated the garden, it would have been different; but he never tidied the place at all. His yard and stable were so littered with things he threw down that you couldn't move about.

It's too bad that some of the people who bought ice from him didn't come and look at how he treated his animals. In the spring and summer he drove them out to pasture, but during the winter they stood day and night in the dark, dirty stable, where the cracks in the wall were so big that the snow swept in almost like drifts. The ground was always muddy and wet, and there was only one small window on the west side where the sun shone in for a short time in the afternoon.

They were very unhappy animals, but they never complained; though sometimes they must have nearly frozen in the bitter winds that blew through the stable on winter nights. Besides being cold they were not well-fed. They were lean and poor, and were never in good health.

Jenkins used to come home almost every afternoon with a great tub in the back of his cart that was full of "peelings." It was kitchen stuff that he asked the cooks at the different houses where he delivered ice to save for him. They threw decayed vegetables, fruit parings, and scraps from the table into the tub, and gave them to him at the end of a few days. A sour, nasty mess it was, not fit for any creature.

Sometimes, when he didn't have enough "peelings," he would go to town and get a load of rotting vegetables that grocers were glad to have taken off their hands, to feed to his animals.

As a result the cows gave very little milk, and Toby the horse was weak and skinny.

2

The Rescue

Jenkins had to start out early in the morning in order to supply his customers, and he was always in a foul temper when he came into the stable in the mornings before the sun was up.

He would hang his lantern on a hook, and if the cows did not step aside just to suit him, he would seize a broom or fork and beat them cruelly.

My mother and I slept on a heap of straw in the corner of the stable, and when she heard his step in the morning she always roused me, so that we could run out as soon as he opened the stable door. He always aimed a kick as we passed, but my mother was careful to teach me how to dodge him.

After he finished milking and a few other chores, he took the milk up to the house for Mrs. Jenkins. Then he came back and harnessed his horse to the cart. Toby was a poor, miserable, broken-down creature. He was weak in the knees, and weak in the back, and weak all over, and Jenkins had to beat him all the time to make him go. His mouth had been jerked, and twisted, and sawed at so much you would think there could be no feeling left; but still I have seen him wince and curl up his lip when Jenkins thrust in the bit in the morning.

Poor old Toby! It's a wonder he didn't cry out with pain. He was cold and starved in the winter time, with raw sores on his body that Jenkins would try to hide by putting bits of cloth under the harness. But Toby never murmured, and never tried to kick and bite. He minded every word from Jenkins, and if he swore at him, Toby would start back, or step up quickly, he was so anxious to please him.

Jenkins had to pick up the ice before starting on his rounds. My mother, Jess, always went with him.

I did not go with her, but watched her until she was out of sight, and then ran up to the house to see if Mrs. Jenkins had any scraps for me. She nearly always was able to save a little something that I could have.

My mother was weak and tired, and though only four years old, seemed much older. This was because of the pitiful amount of poor food that Jenkins fed her. One day she was too weak to run after him, and she lay on our heap of straw, only turning over with her nose the scraps of food I brought her to eat. The next day she licked me gently, wagged her tail, and died.

As I sat by her, grief-stricken and miserable, Jenkins came into the stable. I could not bear to look at him. He had killed my mother. There she lay, a little, gaunt, scarred creature, starved and worried to death by him. Her mouth was half open, her eyes were staring. She would never again look kindly at me, or curl up to me at night to keep me warm. Oh, how I hated him! But I sat quietly, even when he went up and turned her over with his foot to see if she was really dead. I think he was a little sorry, for he turned scornfully toward me and said: "She was worth two of you; why didn't you die instead?"

Still I kept quiet till he walked up to me and kicked at me. My heart was nearly broken and I could stand no more. I flew at him and gave him a savage bite on the ankle.

"Oho," he said, "so you're going to be a fighter, are you? I'll fix that." His face was red and furious. He seized me by the back of the neck and dragged me out to the yard where a tree stump was. "Bert," he called to one of his children, "bring me the hatchet."

He jammed my head on the stump; there was a quick, dreadful pain as he cut off my ears, and turning me around swiftly, though I struggled desperately, cut off my tail close to my body.

Then he let me go, and stood looking at me as I rolled on the ground and yelped in agony. He was in such a fury that he did not realize that people passing by on the road could hear me.

A young man riding by on his bicycle heard my screams, and springing off his bike, came running up the path yelling, "What do you think you're doing to that dog?"

"It's none of your business," said Jenkins.

"Abusing a poor animal is everybody's business," the young man shouted.

And in an instant, he had seized Jenkins by the collar, and was shaking him. Mrs. Jenkins was standing in the doorway crying, but made no effort to help her husband.

"Bring me a towel," the young man yelled at her, after he had knocked Jenkins aside, where he lay frightened on the ground. She pulled off her apron, and gave it to the young man who wrapped me in it. Then taking me carefully in his arms, he walked down the path to the gate.

There were some little boys standing, watching with their mouths wide open in astonishment. He said to the largest of them, "if you will follow me with my bicycle I'll give you a reward."

The boy picked up the bike, and we set out. I was all gathered up in the apron and moaning with pain, but I still looked out occasionally to see which way we were going. We took the road to town, and stopped in front of a house on Washington Street. The young man took some money from his pocket and gave it to the boy. Then he carried me gently up the lane leading to the back of the house.

There was a small stable there, and he went inside and put me down on the floor, and uncovered my body. Some boys were playing in the stable and when they saw us one of them said in a horrified voice, "Oh! Harry, what's the matter with that dog?" "Hush," he said. "Don't make a fuss. Jack, go down to the kitchen and get a basin of warm water and a sponge, and don't let your mother or Laura hear you."

A few minutes later, the young man bathed my bleeding ears and tail, rubbed something on them that was cool and pleasant, and bandaged them firmly with strips of cotton tape. I felt a little better, and was able to look around.

It was a small stable, used more for a play-room. There were various toys scattered about, and a swing and cross-bar, such as kids love to twist about on. In a box against the wall was a guinea pig looking at me in an interested way. A long-haired French rabbit was hopping about, and a tame white rat was perched on the shoulder of one of the boys. He stared hard at me with his little red eyes. Out in the sunny yard, some pigeons were pecking at grain, and a spaniel lay asleep by the fence. While I was puzzling over this, one of the boys cried out, "Here comes Laura!"

A young girl, holding up one hand to shade the sun, was coming up the walk that led from the house to the stable, where I stood in the doorway. "Why, what a funny dog," she said, and stopped short to look at me. Knowing I was not a fit spectacle, I slunk into a corner.

"Poor doggie, have I hurt your feelings?" she said, and came up to the guinea pig's box, behind which I had taken refuge. "What is the matter with your head, good dog?" she said curiously, as she stooped over me.

She drew back, and turned very pale. "Harry, there are drops of blood on this cotton. What has happened to this dog?"

"Laura," the young man said, coming up to her and laying his hand on her shoulder, "he's been hurt, and I have been bandaging him."

"I wish to know who hurt him." Her voice was gentle, but she spoke so decidedly that the young man felt obliged to tell her.

When he had finished his account of rescuing me from Jenkins, she said quietly, "You will have the man punished?"

"What's the use? That won't stop him from being cruel."

"It will put a check on his cruelty. Harry," and the young girl stood up very straight and tall, her brown eyes flashing, with one hand pointing at me; "That animal has been wronged and the coward who has maimed it for life should be punished. A child has a voice to cry for help - a poor animal must suffer in silence; in bitter, bitter silence. And," she said eagerly, as the young man tried to interrupt her, "you are doing the man himself an injustice. If he is bad enough to ill-treat his dog, he will ill-treat his wife and children. If he is checked and punished now for his cruelty, he may reform. And even if his wicked heart is not changed, he will be obliged to treat them with outward kindness, through fear of punishment."

The young man looked convinced. "What do you want me to do?" "I want you to report that man immediately. I will go down to the police station with you, if you like."

"Very well," he said, his face brightening. And together they went off to the house.

3

Adding to My Name

The boys watched them go out of sight, then one of them, named Jack, gave a low whistle and said, "She sure comes on strong when anyone or anything gets hurt! It's lucky for that dog that Harry is visiting us. I think he's taking a shine to Laura too. Did you see the way he looked at her when she suggested going with him to report that man?"

Then they all came over to look at me, as I lay on the floor in the corner. I wasn't used to boys, and didn't know how they would treat me. But I soon found out by the way they handled me and talked to me that they knew a great deal about dogs, and were accustomed to treating them kindly. It seemed very strange to have them pat me and call me "good dog." No one had ever said that to me before.

"He's not much of a beauty, is he?" said one of the boys, named Ned.

"Not by a long shot," said Jack, with a laugh. "What did Harry say the dog's name was?"

"Joe," answered another boy. "The little boy that brought the bicycle home told me his name."

"Maybe we should call him 'Ugly Joe' then," said Carl. "No, I don't think Laura would like that. If we call him 'Ugly Joe' she will say that we're hurting the dog's feelings. 'Beautiful Joe' would be more to her liking."

A shout went up from the boys. "'Beautiful Joe' then, let it be!" they shouted. "Let's go tell mother, and ask her to give us something for our beauty to eat."

They soon brought food, but I couldn't touch it, so they went away to play. While I lay in my box, trembling with pain, I wished the pretty lady was there to stroke me with her gentle fingers.

After awhile it got dark. The boys finished playing and went into the house, and I saw lights twinkling in the windows. I felt lonely and miserable in this strange place.

The pain all through my body was dreadful. My head seemed to be on fire, and there were sharp, darting pains up and down my backbone. I didn't dare howl, lest I disturb the big dog sleeping in a kennel out in the yard.

The stable was very quiet. Up in the loft above, some rabbits had gone to sleep. The guinea pig was nestling in the corner of his box, and the cat and the tame rat had scampered into the house long ago.

At last I could bear the pain no longer, and sat up in my box and looked about. I felt as if I were going to die, and though I was very weak, I wanted to crawl away somewhere out of sight. I slunk out into the yard and along the stable wall, where there was a thick clump of raspberry bushes. I crept in among them and lay down on the damp earth. I tried to scratch off my bandages, but they were fastened on too firmly. I thought about my poor mother, and wished she were there. In the midst of my trouble I heard a soft voice calling, "Joe! Joe!" It felt as if there were weights on my paws, so I couldn't go to her.

"Jo – oe!" she said again. She was going along the walk to the stable, holding a light in her hand.

I watched her till she disappeared in the stable. She did not stay in there long. She came out and stood on the gravel. "Beautiful Joe, where are you? You're hiding somewhere, but I will find you." Then she came right to the spot where I was. "Poor dog," she said, stooping down and patting me. "Are you very miserable, and did you crawl away to die? I'm not going to let you die, Joe." And she set her light on the ground and took me in her arms.

I was very thin then, not nearly so big as I am now; still I was quite an armful for her. But she did not seem to find me heavy. She took me right into the house, through the back door, and into the kitchen.

"Why, Laura," said the woman bending near the stove, "what have you got there?"

"A poor, sick dog, mother," said Laura. "Let's warm a little milk for him, and is there a box or a basket around that he can lie in?"

"We'll find something, but he's awfully dirty"

"He is very ill, and a dreadful thing happened to him, mother," and Laura went on to tell her how my ears and tail had been cut off.

"Oh, that's the dog the boys were talking about, the poor creature."

She opened a closet door and brought out a box, and folded a piece of blanket for me to lie on. While Laura heated some milk in a saucepan and poured it in a saucer, her mother went upstairs to get a little bottle of medicine that would make me sleep. She poured a few drops of this into the milk and offered it to me. I lapped a little, but I couldn't finish it, even though Laura coaxed me very gently. So she dipped her finger in the milk and held it out to me, and though I did not want it, I could not be ungrateful enough to refuse to lick her finger as often as she offered it to me. After the milk was gone, she carried me into the laundry room, and soon I fell sound asleep. I did not stir through the entire night.

4

My New Home

A dog couldn't wish for a happier home than I had now. In a week,
thanks to good nursing, good food and kind words, I was almost well. Harry
washed and dressed my sore ears and tail every day till he went home, and
one day he and the boys gave me a bath in the stable. They carried out a tub
of warm water and stood me in it. I had never been washed before in my life,
and it felt very strange. Laura stood by laughing and encouraging me not to
mind the streams of water trickling all over me. I wonder what Jenkins
would have said if he could have seen me in that tub.

My wonderful new family were called the Morris family. There was Mr.
Morris, who was a clergyman and preached in a church in Fairport, Mrs.
Morris, his wife; Laura, who was the eldest child of the family, then Jack,
Ned and Carl.

Two days after I arrived, Jack, followed by the other boys, came running into the stable carrying a newspaper, and with a great deal of laughing and joking read this to me:

"*Fairport Daily News*, June 3rd. In the police court this morning, James Jenkins was sentenced for cruelly torturing and mutilating a dog, and was fined one hundred dollars plus costs."

Then he said, "What do you think of that, Joe? But there's more, old fellow. Listen: 'Our reporter visited the house of the above mentioned Jenkins and found a most deplorable state of affairs. The house, yard, and stable were indescribably filthy. His horse bears the marks of ill usage and is in a pitiful condition. His cows are plastered with mud and filth, and are covered with vermin. Upon investigation it was found that the man Jenkins has a very bad character and had also been abusing his wife and children, so steps are being taken to have his wife and children removed from him, and his animals given new homes."

Jack threw the paper into my box, and he and the other boys gave three cheers for the *Fairport Daily News* and then ran away. How glad I was! It didn't matter so much about me, for I had escaped him, but now that it was known what a cruel man he was, there would be restraints on him, and perhaps poor Toby and the cows would have a happier time, and his wife and children would be safe.

5

My New Friend

One day a carriage drove up to the house and a finely dressed woman named Mrs. Montague got out, and came up the steps. Mrs. Morris seemed glad to see her, and called her Louise. I went and sat on the rug by the fireplace quite near her.

"I beg your pardon, Jane," she said, "but that is a very strange looking dog you have there."

"Yes," said Mrs. Morris quietly' "he's not a handsome dog."

"And he's new, isn't he?" said Mrs. Montague.

"Yes."

"And that makes ..."

"Two dogs, a cat, fifteen or twenty rabbits, a rat, about a dozen canaries, and two dozen goldfish; I don't know how many pigeons, a few bantam roosters, a guinea pig, and - well, I don't think there are any more."

They both laughed, and Mrs. Montague said: "Quite a menagerie."

"It is," said Mrs. Morris, "and haven't I heard that your son Charlie wants a dog?"

"Oh," cried the lady, with a little shudder, "I hope not. I hate dogs."

"Why do you hate them?" asked Mrs. Morris gently.

"They are so dirty; they always smell and have fleas."

"A dog," said Mrs. Morris, "is something like a child. If you want it clean and pleasant, you must keep it so. This dog's skin is as clean as yours or mine. Hold still, Joe," and she brushed the hair on my back the wrong way to show Mrs. Montague how pink and clean my skin was.

Mrs. Montague looked at me more kindly, and even held out the tips of her fingers to me. Still looking a little uncertain, she asked Mrs. Morris: "But why do you want so many animals?"

Mrs. Morris was quiet for a moment, then replied: "They have been such a wonderful help to me in bringing up my children. We bought this house because it had a large garden, and a stable with room for the boys to play and keep a few animals. But as time went by, I was not really pleased with the way things were going. The boys did nothing for anyone but themselves from morning to night. If I wanted them to do an errand for me, it was done unwillingly. One day I gathered them together and asked them if they thought they were going to make really kind, helpful boys at this rate, and they said no. So I suggested the idea of having pets. They were very enthusiastic, so I brought home a pair of rabbits for Jack, a pair of canaries for Carl and pigeons for Ned. They were delighted with my choices, and scurried about to provide food and shelter for their new pets. They have taken good care of them, and found much pleasure in doing so ever since. The end of it all is, that my boys, in caring for these creatures, have become unselfish and thoughtful. They would rather go to school without their own breakfast than have the inhabitants of the stable go hungry. They are getting an education of the heart, which adds to the intellectual education they're getting at school.

While Mrs. Morris was talking, her visitor leaned forward in her chair and listened attentively. When she finished, Mrs. Montague said quietly: "Thank you, I'm glad you told me this story. I shall get Charlie a dog."

"I am pleased to hear you say that," replied Mrs. Morris. "It will be a good thing for your little boy. A child can learn many lessons from a dog. "This one," pointing to me, "might be held up as an example to many human beings. He is patient, quiet and obedient, but he came to us from a very unhappy home," and Mrs. Morris went on to tell her friend what she knew of my early days.

When she stopped, Mrs. Montague's face was shocked and pained. "How dreadful to think that there are such creatures as that man Jenkins in the world."

Still looking dazed, she got up to leave.

After saying good-by, she stooped down to pat me, walked down the steps and drove away.

Two days later her little boy Charlie came to the house with a present for me. Mrs. Morris opened it, and there was a handsome, nickel-plated collar, with my name on it - *Beautiful Joe*. They took off the shabby leather strap that the boys had given me when I came, and fastened on my new collar, and then Mrs. Morris held me up to a mirror to look at myself. I felt that with such a fine collar I could hold my head up high with any dog.

"Look at you, dear Joe," said Mrs. Morris, pressing my head tightly between her hands.

I felt very grateful to Mrs. Montague for my new collar, and afterward, when I met her in the street, I paused and looked at her. Sometimes she saw me and stopped her carriage to speak to me; but I always wagged my tail, or rather my body, for I had no tail to wag, whenever I saw her, whether she saw me or not.

A few days later her little boy, Charlie, his eyes shining, came over to show Laura and her brothers his beautiful new Irish setter, "Brisk."

6

The Fox-Terrier Skippy

One day while I was sitting beside Laura in the parlor, the door opened, and her brother came in. One of his hands was laid over the other, and he said to his sister, "Guess what I've got here?"

"A bird," she said.

"No."

"A rat."

"No."

"A mouse."

"No, it's a pup."

"Oh, Jack," she said doubtfully.

He opened his hands, and there lay the tiniest morsel of a fox-terrier puppy. He was white, with black and tan markings. His body was pure white, his tail black, with a dash of tan; his ears black, and his face evenly marked with black and tan. You could not tell the color of his eyes, as they were not open. Later on, they turned out to be a pretty brown.

His nose was pale pink, and when he got older it became jet black.

"Why, Jack!" exclaimed Laura, "his eyes aren't open; why did you take him from his mother?"

"She's dead," said Jack. "Poisoned. She left her pups to run about the yard for a little exercise. Some brute had thrown over a piece of poisoned meat, and she ate it. Four of the pups died. This is the only one left. Mr. Robinson says he doesn't understand about raising pups without their mother. He wants us to have it because he thinks we're so good at nursing sick animals."

Laura took the tiny creature and went upstairs very thoughtfully. I followed her, and watched her get a little basket and line it with cotton wool. She put the puppy in it, and looked at him. Though it was midsummer, and the house seemed very warm to me, the little creature was shivering, and making a low, murmuring noise. She pulled the fabric over him, shut the window, and set his basket in the sun.

Then she went to the kitchen for some warm milk. She dipped her finger in it, and offered it to the puppy, but he went nosing about and wouldn't touch it. "Too young," Laura said. She got a piece of muslin, put some bread in it and dipped it in the milk. When she put this to the puppy's mouth, he sucked it greedily. He acted as if he were starving, but Laura only let him have a little.

Every few hours, for the rest of the day, she gave him some more milk, and for many nights she got up once or twice and heated milk for him. No one seemed to think it was too much trouble to take care of a creature that was nothing but a dog.

He fully repaid them for all this care because he turned out to be one of the prettiest and most lovable dogs around. He was very amusing when he was a puppy. He was full of tricks, and crept about in a mischievous way when you didn't know he was near. He was very small, and used to climb inside Laura's jersey sleeve up to her shoulder. One day, when the whole family was in the parlor, Mr. Morris suddenly flung aside his newspaper and began jumping up and down.

"There's a rat up my leg," he said, shaking it violently. Just then little Skippy fell out on the floor and lay on his back looking up at Mr. Morris with a suprised face. He had felt cold and thought it would be warm inside Mr. Morris' trousers leg.

Skippy never did any real mischief, thanks to Laura's training. She began to train him just as soon as he began to tear and chew things. The first thing he attacked was Mr. Morris' felt hat. The wind blew it down the hall one day, and Skippy came along and began to chew on it.

Laura found him, and he rolled his eyes at her quite innocently, not knowing that he was doing wrong. She took the hat away, and pointing from it to him, said, "No, Skippy." Then she gave him two or three slaps with a shoelace. She never struck a little dog with her hand or a stick. She said this was a better way to scold them, for a good dog feels a severe scolding as much as a whipping.

Skippy was very much ashamed of himself and nothing could get him to look at a hat again. But he thought there was no harm in chewing other things. He attacked one thing after another: shoes, books, the rugs on the floor, curtains, anything flying or fluttering; and Laura patiently scolded him for each one, till at last it dawned upon him that he must not chew anything but a bone. Then he grew up to be a very good dog.

There was one thing that Laura was very particular about, and that was to feed him regularly. He was given three meals a day while he was a puppy.

We were never allowed to go into the dining room, and while the family was at the table we lay in the hall outside and watched what was going on.

As soon as dinner was over, Skippy and I scampered after Laura to the kitchen. Each one had his own plate for food. Mother often laughed at Laura because she would not let her dogs "dish" together. Laura said that if she did, the larger one would get more than his share, and the little one would starve.

It was quite a sight to watch Skippy eat. He spread his legs apart to steady himself, and gobbled up his food like a duck. When he finished he always looked up for more, and Laura would shake her head and say: "No, Skippy, you've had enough."

I must not forget to say that Skippy was washed regularly, once a week with nice smelling soap, and once a month with stronger soap. He had his own towels and wash cloths, and after being rubbed and scrubbed he was rolled in a blanket and put by the fire to dry.

Rusty, the Morris's other dog, and I were hardier than Skippy, and took our baths in the sea. Every few days the boys took us down to the shore, and we went swimming with them.

7

Training a Puppy

"Ned, dear," Laura said one day, "I wish you would train Skippy to follow and retrieve. He is four months old now, and I shall soon want to take him out on the street."

"Well, okay," said mischievous Ned, and grabbing a stick he said, "Come out into the garden, dogs."

Though he was brandishing his stick very fiercely, I was not at all afraid of him; and as for Skippy, he loved Ned.

The Morris garden was really not a garden, but a large piece of ground with the grass worn bare in many places, a few trees scattered about, and some raspberry and currant bushes along the edge.

Ned walked around and around the yard, with his stick on his shoulder, Skippy and I strolling after him. Skippy made a dash aside to get a bone he left in the yard earlier. Ned turned around and said firmly, "Heel."

Skippy looked at him innocently, not knowing what he meant. "Heel!" exclaimed Ned again. Skippy thought he wanted to play, and putting his head on his paws, he began to bark. Ned laughed, still he kept saying, "heel." He would not say another word. He knew if he said, "Come here," or "Follow," or "Go behind," it would confuse Skippy.

Finally, as Ned kept saying the word over and over, and pointing to me, it seemed to dawn upon Skippy that he wanted Skippy to follow him. So he came beside me, and together we followed Ned around the garden, again and again.

After a snack, he called us out into the garden again, and said he had something else to teach us. He sat on the wooden platform at the back door, and then called Rusty to him.

He took a small leather strap from his pocket. It had a nice, strong smell. We all licked it, and each dog wished to have it. "No, Joe and Skippy," said Ned, holding us both by our collars, "you wait a minute. Here, Rusty."

Rusty watched him very earnestly, and Ned threw the strap half-way across the garden and said, "Fetch it."

Rusty never moved till he heard the words, "Fetch it." Then he ran swiftly, brought the strap, and dropped it in Ned's hand. Ned sent him after it two or three times, then he said to Rusty, "Sit," and turned to me. "Here, Joe, it's your turn."

He threw the strap under the raspberry bushes, then looked at me and said, "Fetch it." I knew quite well what he meant, and ran joyfully after it. I soon found it by the strong smell, but once I got it in my mouth, I began to gnaw it and play with it, and when Ned called out: "Fetch it," I dropped it and ran toward him.

Ned pointed to the place where it was and spread out his empty hands. That helped me, and I ran quickly and got it. He made me get it for him several times. Sometimes I could not find it right away, and sometimes I dropped it, but he never stirred. He sat still till I brought it to him. Soon I learned.

It was kindness and patience that did it. When I was with Jenkins he thought I was a very stupid dog. He would have laughed at the idea of anyone teaching me anything. But I was only sullen and obstinate because I was kicked about so much. If he had been kind to me, I would have done anything for him.

8

The Parrot Bella

The Morrises used to speak about ships that sailed between Fairport and the West Indies, carrying cargoes of lumber and fish, and bringing home molasses, spices, fruit, and other things. On one of these vessels was a cabin-boy, who was a friend of the Morris boys, and he often brought them presents.

One day, he arrived at the house with a bunch of green bananas in his arms and a parrot on his shoulder. The boys were delighted with the parrot, and called their mother to come see what a pretty bird she was.

Mrs. Morris seemed very touched by the boy's thoughtfulness in bringing a present such a long distance, and thanked him warmly.

Jack put me up on the table to look at the parrot. The boy held her by a string tied around one of her legs. She was a gray parrot with a few red feathers in her tail, and she had bright eyes, and a very knowing air.

The boy said he had been careful to buy a young one that could not speak, for he knew the Morris boys would not want one chattering in a foreign language.

He had kept her in his bunk on the ship, and had spent all his leisure time teaching her to talk. Then he looked at her anxiously, and said, "Show off now, okay, Bella?"

I stood on the table staring hard at her, and she stared hard at me. I heard someone say, "Beautiful Joe." The voice seemed to come from the room, but I knew all the voices there, and this was one I had never heard before, so I thought I must be mistaken. I struggled to get away from Jack, to run and see who it was. But he held me fast, and laughed with all his might. I looked at the other boys and they were laughing too. Then I heard it again, "Beau-ti-ful Joe, Beau-ti-ful Joe." The sound was close by, and yet it did not come from the cabin-boy, for he was doubled up laughing.

"It's the parrot, Joe," cried Ned. "Look at her. He's spent hours teaching her to say things about this family.

I did look at her, and with her head cocked to one side, and the sauciest air in the world, she was saying, "Beau-ti-ful Joe!"

I tried to get down and hide under the table. Then she began to laugh at me. "Ha, ha, ha, good dog, sic 'em, boy. Rats! Rats! Beau-ti-ful Joe, Beau-ti-ful Joe," she cried, rattling off the words as fast as she could.

The boys roared with delight at my puzzled face. Then the parrot began calling for Rusty: "Where's Rusty, where's good old Rusty? Poor old dog. Give him a bone." The boys brought Rusty in, and when he heard her funny little cracked voice calling him, he nearly went crazy: "Rusty, Rusty, Rusty Augustus!" she said, which was Rusty's full name.

He made a dash out of the room, and the boys shouted so loud that Mr. Morris came down from his study to see what was happening. As soon as the parrot saw him, she would not utter another word. The boys told him, though, what she had been saying, and he seemed much amused to think that the cabin-boy should have remembered so many of his boys' expressions, and taught them to the parrot.

The next day, the boys bought a fine, large cage for her. She hated her cage, and used to put her head close to the bars and plead: "Let Bella out; Bella will be a good girl. "

After a time, the Morrises did let her out, and she kept her word and never tried to run away. Jack put a little handle on her cage door so that she could open and shut it herself. It was very amusing to hear her say in the morning, "Clear the track, children! Bella's going to take a walk," and see her turn the handle with her claw and come out into the room. She was a very clever bird, and got to know a good deal of English.

9

Justice Triumphs

The first winter I was with the Morrises, a strange coincidence happened. It was the week before Christmas, and we were having cold, frosty weather. Not much snow had fallen, but there was plenty of skating, and the boys were off every day with their skates on a little lake near Fairport.

Rusty and I often went with them, and we had great fun scampering over the ice and slipping at every step.

On this Saturday night we had just come home. It was quite dark outside, and there was a cold wind blowing, so when we came in the front door, and saw the blazing fire in the living room, it looked very welcome and cheerful.

This was the cosiest time of day, with the family all sitting around the fire: Mrs. Morris sewing, the boys reading or studying, Mr. Morris with his head buried in a newspaper, and Skippy and I on the floor at their feet.

That evening I was feeling very drowsy, and had almost fallen asleep when Ned gave me a little nudge with his foot. He was a great tease, and he delighted in getting me to make a simpleton of myself. I tried to keep my eyes on the fire, but I could not, and just had to turn and look at him.

He was holding his book up between himself and his mother so she couldn't see him and was opening his mouth as wide as he could and throwing back his head, pretending to howl.

I could not help giving a loud howl. Mrs. Morris looked up and said, "No Joe, be quiet."

The boys were all laughing behind their books, for they knew what Ned was doing. Soon he started off again and I was just beginning another howl that might have made Mrs. Morris send me out of the room, when the door opened and a young girl called Bessie Drury came in.

She had just run across the street from her parent's house. "Oh! Mrs. Morris," she said, "will you let Laura come over and stay with me tonight? Mother has just had a telegram from Bangor saying that her aunt is very ill. She wants to see her so father is going to take her there tonight. She's afraid I'll be lonely if I don't have Laura stay with me."

"Yes," said Mrs. Morris, "I'm sure Laura would be happy to go."

"Yes indeed," said Laura, smiling at her friend. "I will come over in half an hour."

"Oh thank you," said Bessie, and she hurried away.

After she left, Mr. Morris looked up from his paper. "There will be some one in the house besides those two girls?"

"Oh, yes," said Mrs. Morris; "Mrs. Drury has her nurse who has been with her for twenty years, and there is the housekeeper, so they will be fine."

"Good," said Mr. Morris, and he went back to his paper.

When Laura came downstairs with her bag, I got up and stood near her. "Good old Joe," she said, "you can't come this time."

I pushed myself out the door beside her after she had kissed her family goodnight. "Go back, Joe," she said firmly.

I had to step back then, but I barked and whined, and she looked at me in astonishment. "I shall be back in the morning, Joe," she said gently. "Please don't whimper like that." Then she left.

I felt terrible and paced up and down the floor, and ran to the window and howled. Mrs. Morris peered over her glasses at me in utter surprise. "Boys," she said, "have you ever seen Joe act this way before?"

"No, mother," they all replied.

Mr. Morris was looking at me very intently. I ran up and put my paws on his knees. "Mother," he said, turning to his wife, "let the dog go."

"Very well," she said in a puzzled way. "Jack, just run over with him, and tell Mrs. Drury how he's acting, and that I shall be very much obliged if she will let him stay all night with Laura."

Jack sprang up, and we raced down the front steps, across the street, through the gate, and up the frozen gravel walk.

The Drury's lived in a big, beautiful house, surrounded by gardens. They didn't keep dogs, or pets of any kind, so Rusty and I never had any excuse to call there.

Jack and I were soon at their front door, and he rang the bell and handed me over to the housekeeper who opened it. The girl listened to his message for Mrs. Drury, then walked upstairs smiling, and glancing at me over her shoulder.

There was a suitcase in the upper hall, and an elderly woman was putting clothes in it. She gave a little scream: "Where did that dog come from? Put him out at once!"

I stood quite still, and the girl who had brought me upstairs gave her Jack's message.

"Oh, all right then," said the lady, when the housekeeper finished speaking. "If he's one of the Morris dogs, he is sure to be well-behaved. Tell the little boy to thank his mother for letting Laura come over, and say that we will keep the dog with pleasure. Now, we must hurry; the cab will be here in five minutes." I walked softly into the living room and found Laura.

There was a scene of great confusion and hurry, but in a few minutes it was all over. The taxi had rolled away, and the house was quiet.

"Susan, is supper ready," said Bessie, "and is there something for Beautiful Joe? I think he would like some of that turkey left from last night's dinner."

What fun we had over our supper! The two girls sat at the big dining table, and sipped their chocolate, and laughed and talked, and I had turkey on a newspaper that Susan had spread on the carpet.

I was very careful not to drag it about, and Bessie laughed at me till tears came to her eyes. "That dog is a gentleman," she said; "see how he holds the turkey on the paper with his paws. Oh, Joe, you are a funny dog! And you are having a funny supper. I have heard of quail on toast, but never of turkey on newspaper."

"The hall clock struck eleven, and Bessie said, "Time for bed. Where is this animal to sleep?"

"I don't know," said Laura; "he sleeps in the stable at home, or in the kennel with Rusty."

"Suppose we make him a nice bed by the kitchen stove?" said Bessie.

They made the bed, but I was not willing to sleep in it. I barked so loudly when they shut me up alone, that they had to let me go upstairs with them.

Laura was almost angry with me, but I couldn't help it. I had come to protect her, and I didn't want to leave her.

Just before Laura dropped off to sleep, she forgave me, and put down her hand for me to lick as I lay on a rug close to her bed.

I was very tired, and as I had a very pleasant bed, I soon fell asleep. There was a big clock in the hall though, and every time it struck, I jumped out of a sound nap. I sprang up, then took a turn around the room.

I went back to my rug and tried to go to sleep, but I could not. I felt uneasy so I started walking about.

The Drury's carpets were like velvet, and my paws didn't make a rattling on them as they did on the tile in the Morris house. I crept down the stairs like a cat, and walked along the lower hall, smelling under all the doors, listening as I went. There was no night light burning down here, and it was quite dark. I was suprised when I got near the far end of the hall to see a tiny

gleam of light shine for an instant from under the dining room door. Then it went away.

I went and sniffed under the door. There was a smell there, a strong smell. It smelled like Jenkins. It *was* Jenkins!

I thought I would go crazy. I scratched at the door, and barked and yelped. I sprang at it. It seemed to me that I would go mad if I couldn't get that door open. Every few seconds I stopped and put my head down to the doorsill to listen. There was a rushing about inside the room, and a chair fell over, and someone seemed to be getting out of the window.

This made me even more frantic.

In the midst of the noise I was making, there was screaming and a rushing to and fro upstairs. I started to run up and down the hall.

"The dog has gone mad," cried Bessie, "pour some water on him."

Susan was more sensible. She ran downstairs, her night gown flying, flung open the front door and started screaming, "Help! Police! There are thieves in the house," she shouted at the top of her voice, "the dog has found it out."

I dashed by her, out the hall door, and away down to the gate, where I heard someone running. I gave a few loud yelps to call Rusty, and leaped the gate to chase Jenkins. There was something fierce in me that night.

Rusty soon caught up with me. We raced after my old enemy, and at the corner caught up with the miserable man.

With an angry growl I jumped on Jenkins to try to stop him. He turned around, and though it was not a very bright night, there was light enough for me to see the ugly face of my old master.

He was furious. He picked up some rocks, and threw them at us. Then we heard the sound of whistles, one in front of us and one behind. Jenkins made a strange noise in his throat, and started to run down a side street, away from the direction of the whistles.

I was afraid that he was going to get away, and though I could not hold him, I kept springing up on him, and once I tripped him. He kicked me against the side of a wall, and gave me two or three hard blows with a stick he had picked up.

Old Rusty got so angry whenever Jenkins hit me that he ran up behind and nipped his calves, to make him turn away from me.

Soon Jenkins came to a stone wall, where he stopped, and with a hurried look behind, began to climb over it. He was going to escape.

I barked as loudly as I could, hoping someone would come, and then sprang up and held onto him by the leg as he was scrambling over the wall.

I had such a grip on him, that we went over the wall together and left Rusty on the other side. Jenkins fell to the ground. Then he got up, and with a look of deadly hatred on his face, jumped on me.

If help had not come, I think he would have killed me. But just then there was the the sound of feet running. Two policemen came down the street to where Rusty was leaping up and down and barking in distress.

In one short instant they had hold of Jenkins. He gave up then, but stood snarling at me in an ugly manner. "If it hadn't been for that mutt, I'd never been caught."

"Why," he staggered back and uttered, "it's me own dog."

"What have you been up to at this time of night?" one of the policemen asked sternly, "to have your own dog and another chasing you through the street?" Jenkins began to swear and would not say any more.

There was a house nearby, and just at this moment someone in an upper room opened a window and called out, "What's going on down there?"

"We're catching a thief, sir," said one of the policemen, snapping a pair of hand-cuffs on Jenkins as he lead him through the gate.

One policeman took Jenkins off to jail while the other one started down the street toward Bessie's house.

"Good dogs," said the policeman to Rusty and me.

As we hurried along Washington Street, and came near our house, we saw lights shining through the darkness, and heard people running back and forth. The nurse's shrieking had alarmed the whole neighborhood. The Morris boys were all out in the street only half clad and shivering with cold.

The neighbors' houses were all lit up, and a good many people were hanging out of their windows and opening their doors, and calling to each other to find out what all the noise meant.

When one of the policeman appeared, quite a crowd gathered around him to hear his story. Rusty and I dropped on the ground panting as hard as we could, with little streams of water running from our tongues. We were both exhausted. Rusty's back was bleeding in several places from the rocks that Jenkins had hit him with, and I was a mass of bruises.

Soon we were discovered, and a great fuss was made over us. "Brave dogs! Good dogs!" everybody said, and patted and praised us. We were very proud and happy, and stood up and wagged our tails, at least Rusty did, and I wagged what I could. Then they found what a state we were in. Mrs. Morris cried, and catching me up in her arms, ran into the house with me, and Jack followed with old Rusty.

We all went into the living room. There was a good fire there, and Laura and Bessie were sitting next to it. They sprang up when they saw us, helped with our injuries, and made us lie down by the fire.

"You saved our silver, brave Joe," said Bessie; "just wait till my mother and father come home and find out."

Suddenly, the Morris boys came running into the room.

"The policeman has been examining the evidence, and has gone down to the station to make his report, and do you know what he has found out?" said Jack excitedly.

"No - what?" asked Bessie.

"Why that villain was going to burn your house down."

Bessie gave a shriek. "Why, what do you mean?"

"Well," said Jack, "they think by what they've discovered, that he planned to pack his bag with silver, then pour oil around the room and set fire to it so that people would not find out that he had been robbing you."

"Why, we might all have burned to death," said Bessie.

"Do you know this for certain, Jack?" asked Laura.

"Well, they think so because they found bottles of oil along with the bag he had for the silver."

"How horrible! You darling old Joe, you saved our lives," and pretty Bessie kissed my ugly, swollen head. I could do nothing but lick her hand.

It is now some years since all this happened, and I might as well tell the end of it. The next day the Drury's came home, and everything was found out about Jenkins. The night they left Fairport he had been hanging around the station. He knew who they were, for he had once supplied them with ice, and knew all about their family. He had no customers at this time, for after Harry rescued me, and that piece came out in the paper about him, he found that no one would take ice from him. His wife had died, and foster parents were taking care of his children, and he was obliged to sell Toby and the cows. Instead of learning from all this and trying to lead a better life, he went from bad to worse.

He was, therefore, ready for some kind of criminal activity, and when he saw the Drurys going away in the train, he thought he would break into their house, look for silver and jewelry to steal, then set a fire to cover his tracks.

He confessed to all this, and was eventually sentenced to prison.

10

Our Journey to Riverdale

Every summer, the Morris children went to visit relatives or friends in the country for a few weeks. As there were so many of them, they usually went to different places.

The children took some of their pets with them, and the others they left at home for their mother to look after. She never allowed them to take a bird or an animal anywhere unless she knew it would be perfectly welcome. "Don't let your pets be a worry to other people," she often said to them, "or they will dislike them and you too."

Laura was going to visit her aunt and uncle in New Hampshire. After my adventure with Jenkins, she said that we should never be parted. If anyone invited her to come and see them, and they didn't want me, she wouldn't go.

This particular year, Laura went away earlier than the others, so the whole family went to the station to see us off. They put a chain on my collar, and took me to the baggage office, and got two tickets for me. One was tied to my collar, and the other Laura put in her purse. Then I was put in a baggage car, and chained in a corner. For a few minutes Laura stood by the door and looked in, but soon the men had piled up so many boxes and trunks that she could not see me. Then she went away. Mr. Morris asked one of the men to look after me, then he too went away.

Before the train started, the doors of the baggage car were closed, and it became dark inside. The darkness, the heat, and the noise as we went rushing along, made me feel sick and frightened.

I did not dare lie down, but sat up trembling and wishing that we might come soon to the Riverdale station. But we did not get there for some time, and I was to have a great fright.

When we began to slacken speed I thought surely we must be at our journey's end. However, it was not Riverdale. The car gave kind of a jump, then there was a crashing sound ahead, and we stopped.

I heard men shouting and running up and down, and wondered what had happened. It was dark and still in the car, and nobody came, but the noise kept up outside, and I knew something had gone wrong with the train. Perhaps Laura had been hurt. Something must have happened to her or she would come for me.

I barked and barked and pulled at my chain till my neck was sore, but for a long, long time I was there alone. The men running about outside must have heard me, because the door at the end of the car finally opened, and a man looked in. "This is all baggage for New York, miss," I heard him say, "they wouldn't put your dog in here." "Yes, they did - I am sure this is the car," I heard in the voice I knew so well, "and will you get him out, please? He must be terribly frightened."

I erupted into a frenzy of jerking on the chain and trying to bark and the man finally found me. He stooped down and unfastened my chain, grumbling to himself that I had not been put in the right car. "Some folks push a dog around as if he were a lump of coal," he said, patting me on the back kindly.

I was nearly wild with delight to be with Laura again, but I had barked so much, and pressed my neck so hard with my collar, that my voice was gone. I fawned on her, and wagged myself about, and opened and shut my mouth, but no sound came out.

It made Laura nervous. She tried to laugh and cry at the same time, and then bit her lip hard, and said, "Oh! Joe, don't."

He's lost his bark, hasn't he?" said the man, looking at me curiously.

"It is a wicked thing to confine an animal in a dark and closed car," said Laura, trying to see her way down the steps through her tears.

The man put out his hand and helped her. Laura, her face very much troubled, picked her way among the bits of coal and wood scattered about the platform, and went into the waiting room of the little station.

She took me to the fountain and let some water run in her hand, and gave it to me to lap. Then she sat down and I leaned my head against her knees, and she stroked my throat gently with her quiet hand.

There had been a freight train on a side track at this station, waiting for us to pass it. The switchman had carelessly left the switch open, and we went crashing into the freight train. Our engine was smashed so badly that it could not take us on, and we were waiting for another engine to come and take us to Riverdale.

Finally, our engine arrived, and as it was only a few miles to Riverdale, the conductor let me stay in the car with Laura. She spread her coat out on the seat in front of her, and I sat on it and looked out of the car window as we sped along through lovely country, all green and fresh in the June sunlight. How light and pleasant this car was - so different from the baggage car. What frightens an animal most of all, is not to see where it's going, not to know what's going to happen to it. They must be very like human beings in this respect.

A lady had taken a seat beside Laura, and as she leaned over to stroke my head, Laura said, "You seem very fond of animals."

"I am, my dear. I have four horses, two cows, a tame squirrel, three dogs, and a cat."

"You should be a very happy woman," said Laura with a smile.

"I don't see how anyone can not love and be kind to animals," said Laura thoughtfully.

"Nor I, my dear child. It has always caused me intense pain to witness the torture of animals. Over sixty years ago, when I was a little girl playing in the streets of Boston, I would tremble and grow faint at the cruelty of drivers to overloaded horses. I was timid and did not dare speak to them. Very often, I ran home and flung myself in my mother's arms in tears, and asked her if nothing could be done to help the poor animals. With mistaken motherly kindness, she tried to put the subject out of my thoughts. But the animals went on suffering just the same, and when I became an adult, I worked very hard on the problem, and was able to assist in the formation of several societies for the prevention of cruelty to animals.

A little child is such a tender thing. You can bend it any way you like. You can teach heart education to children as well as mind education. Many teachers now say that there is nothing better than to give children lessons in kindness to animals. Children who are taught to protect animals will be kind to all those they meet when they grow up.

But, my dear child, here we are at your station. Good bye. Keep your happy face and gentle ways. I hope that we may meet again some day."

She pressed Laura's hand, gave me a farewell pat, and the next minute we were outside on the platform, and she was smiling through the window.

11

Dingley Farm

As we walked toward the station, Laura's aunt rushed up, and threw both arms around Laura. She was a stout, middle-aged woman, with a red, lively face. "How glad I am to see you. And this is the dog I've heard so much about. Good Joe, I have a bone waiting for you. And here's dear Laura, Uncle John."

A tall man stepped up and put out a big hand, in which my mistress' little fingers were quite swallowed up. "I am glad to see you, Laura. Well, Joe, how do you do, old boy?"

It made me feel very welcome to have them both notice me, and I was so glad to be out of the train that I frisked for joy around their feet as we went to the carriage. It was a big double one, with an awning over it for shelter from the sun's rays, and the horses were drawn up in the shade of a spreading tree. They were two powerful black horses, and as they had no blinders on, they could see us coming. Their faces lit up, and they moved their ears, pawed the ground, and whinnied when Mr. Wood went up to them. "Steady there, Cleve, Pacer," he said; "now back, back up."

By this time Mrs. Wood, Laura, and I were in the wagon. Then Mr. Wood jumped in, took up the reins, and off we went.

How the two black horses did spin along! I sat on the seat behind Mr. Wood, and sniffed the delicious air with its lovely smell of flowers and grass. What long runs I should have in the green fields of the country.

We came to a turn in the road where the ground sloped gently upward. We turned in at the gate, and drove between rows of trees up to a long, low, red house, with a veranda all around it. There was a wide lawn in front, and away on our right were the farm buildings. They too were painted red, and there was a row of trees by them that Mr. Wood called his windbreak, because they kept the snow from drifting in the winter time.

"Welcome to Dingley Farm, Laura and Joe," said Mrs. Wood, with her jolly laugh. "Come on in and let's have lunch."

A few days after we arrived Harry came home to visit his mother and stepfather, Mr. Woods. To honor the occasion, the Woods, Harry, Laura, and Mr. Maxwell, president of the local *Band of Mercy* group, had gathered for tea.

Mr. Maxwell was an interesting man who was known for his love of animals and had many pets himself. He had been very active in The Band of Mercy movement, one of the early societies developed to teach people respect for animals.

When Harry saw me, he turned to Laura and said, "What dog is that?" - pointing to me.

"Why, Harry," exclaimed Laura, "don't you recognize Beautiful Joe? You rescued him from that wretched ice man."

"Is it possible," he said, "that this well-conditioned creature is the bundle of dirty skin and bones that we nursed in Fairport? Come here, Joe. Do you remember me?"

Indeed I did remember him, and I licked his hands and looked up gratefully into his face. "You're a handsome fellow now," he said caressing me with a firm, kind hand. "You look like a protector, but I suppose you wouldn't let him fight even if he wanted to, Laura," and he smiled and glanced at her. "No," she said, "I don't think I should, but he can fight when the occasion requires it," and she told him the story of Jenkins.

All the time she was speaking, Harry held me by the paws and stroked my body over and over again. When she finished, he put his head down to me, and murmured, "Good dog," and I saw that his eyes were red and shining.

"That's a wonderful story; we must tell it at the next Band of Mercy meeting," said Mr. Maxwell, "we're very interested in stories showing how noble animals can be."

Mr. Maxwell apparently had a reputation for being forgetful, and this day at tea was no exception. I had caught a glimpse of a strange green creature, with a darting tongue, sticking his head out of his pocket, and I worried about it possibly hurting Laura.

They were all seated around the tea table and Mrs. Wood said, "Perhaps you'll serve the berries and pass the cream and sugar, John. Do you get cream like this in the village, Mr. Maxwell?"

"No, Mrs. Wood," he said, "ours is a much lighter cream." Then there was a great tinkling of china, and passing of dishes, and talking and laughing; and nobody noticed that I was not in my usual place in the hall. I could not get over my dread of the creature, and I crept under the table, so that if it came out and frightened Laura, I could jump up and catch it.

When tea was half over, she gave a little cry. I sprang up, and there, gliding over the table toward her, was the wicked-looking green thing. I stepped onto the table, and had it by its middle before it could get her. One of my hind legs was in a dish of jelly, and one of my front ones was in a plate of cake, and I was very uncomfortable. The tail of the green thing hung in a milk pitcher, and it's tongue was still going at me, but I held it firmly and stood quite still.

"Drop it, Joe, drop it," cried Laura in tones of distress, and Mr. Maxwell struck me on the back, so I let the thing go and stood sheepishly looking about me. Mr. Wood was leaning back in his chair, laughing with all his might, and Mrs. Wood was staring at her untidy table. Laura told me to jump to the floor, and then she helped her aunt take the spoiled things off the table.

I felt that I had done wrong, so I slunk out into the hall. Mr. Maxwell was tearing his handkerchief in strips and tying them around the creature where my teeth had bit in. He scowled at me, saying, "You rascal, you've really hurt my poor snake."

I felt so bad to hear this that I went and stood in a corner. After a while, Mr. Maxwell went back into the room, and they all went on with their tea. I could hear Mr. Wood say in a loud, cheery voice: "The dog did quite right. Some snakes are poisonous creatures, and his instinct told him to protect his mistress. Where is he? Joe, Joe?"

I would not move till Laura came and spoke to me. "Good old Joe," she whispered, "you knew the snake was there all the time, didn't you?"

Her words made me feel better, and I followed her to the dining room, where Mr. Wood made me sit beside him all through the rest of the meal.

Mr. Maxwell had gotten over his ill humor, and was chatting in a lively way. "Good Joe," he said; "I was cross at you, and I beg your pardon. I can't stand to see an animal injured. You couldn't know my poor snake is harmless, and was only looking for something to eat. Mrs. Wood has pinned my pocket so he won't come out again.

All animals need our protection and concern. There is a good deal of talk nowadays about kindness to domestic animals, but I don't hear much about kindness to wild ones. I can't see why you wouldn't protect one as well as the other. We have no more right to abuse a bear than a cow."

Blackjack

One day, after we had returned home to Fairport, the Morris boys were walking in the pinewood near the house and I was trotting ahead of them, when I smelled something alive.

I sniffed about, and there crouching on a heap of pine needles was a featherless young crow.

I barked, and the boys hurried to pick up the little creature. There were no other crows nearby, so they took it home to care for it.

It became Jack's pet, and soon it was old enough to follow him about. Jack fed it worms, bread and milk - according to the Vet's suggestions, and the young bird became a glossy creature with strong wings, a heavy beak, and a voice that used to make me jump when he stole up behind me as I lay sleeping in the sun.

"Our painful pleasure," Laura used to call him, for though she loved him almost as much as her brothers did, he was a great worry to her.

He began by teasing the creatures about the place, especially with regard to their food, until most of them got to understand him so well that they would run if they saw him coming.

The guinea pig, Jeffy, and the rabbits would stick their heads out of the stable door, and if Blackjack was in the garden, they would go back inside.

The tame rat always ran to his friend, Bella, the parrot, for Blackjack was afraid of her saucy tongue.

The pigeons and bantams didn't like him, for when they were out in the garden feeding, he would swoop down among them, and send them flying.

Then, with solemn crow satisfaction, he would eat their grain, taking on a pretended air of penitence when Laura scolded him.

One day he played a shabby trick on Mother. She had bought a fine steak for dinner, and it was on a plate in the pantry window.

Blackjack was eyeing it from a tree, but before anyone knew what was passing through his crow mind, he had swooped down, snatched it and flown it up to the stable roof.

Mother came into the kitchen just in time to witness the theft, and the expression on her face was so comical as she watched Blackjack tearing the family dinner to pieces, that Laura and the boys couldn't help laughing.

Later, I heard Mr. Morris say to Laura: "That crow is out of his sphere. Couldn't you persuade him to join his wild kind in the woods?"

"He's Jack's pet," she replied, "and though he has taken him into the woods, he always comes back."

One day, some wild crows passed overhead, and with a happy "caw," he flew up and joined them.

When night came he didn't return, and I felt sorry for Jack, who looked for his pet all over the neighborhood.

Animals and birds understand each other, but Jack was a human being, and I could not tell him that every drop of wild blood in Blackjack was calling out for his brother and sister crows.

Jack went to bed in great anxiety, for he feared that some mishap had befallen his pet.

We did not see the crow for a week. Then one day as Jack was standing in the garden, there was a rush of wings and Blackjack was on his shoulder, pinching his ear and thrusting his black beak into his young master's face while he chattered about the joys of wild life.

Then he disappeared once more and we did not see him for weeks.

On his second return he was more shy, and would not allow Jack to catch him. On his third, he sat on the stable roof and talked crow very earnestly.

There were several other returns, but he never flew down in the yard again, and finally he disappeared never to return.

The Morrises often discussed Blackjack and wondered if he was okay.

I knew he was alive and well, and had a family of his own in the pinewood. He remembered the Morrises, and if any of the family went into the woods, he cawed affectionately, though he did not go near them.

13

The End of My Story

I have now come to the end of my story. I shall just bring my tale down to the present time, and then stop talking, and go lie down in my basket, for I am an old dog now, and get tired very easily.

I was a year old when I went to the Morris family, and I have been with them for twelve years. I am not living in the same house with them now, but I am with my dear Laura, who is now Mrs. Gray. She fell in love and married Harry four years ago, and lives with him on Dingley Farm. Mr. and Mrs. Morris have retired to a cottage nearby.

When the Morris boys are all here in the summer we have great times together. All through the winter we look forward to their coming, for they make the old farmhouse and yard come alive.

We roam the woods and fields together where the wildflowers nod in the sunshine and the land hums with the sound of bees, and the springs meandering through the meadows make a special music when mixed with the laughter of the boys at play.

They are considerate of my changing fitness as they throw the sticks closer for me to fetch, and wait longer between throws as they bend down and pat me and say, "Way to go, Beautiful Joe, way to go old fellow."

Laura is especially kind to me and I can tell by her looks and the softness of her voice and the touch of her hand that she really loves me, as I love her.

Bella, the parrot, lives with Mrs. Morris, and is as smart as ever. I have heard that parrots live to a very great age. Some of them even get to be a hundred years old. If that's the case, Bella will outlive us all. She notices that I am getting blind and feeble, and when I go down to see Mrs. Morris, she calls out to me: "Keep the game a-going, Beautiful Joe."

Light up the mind of a child

with these animal stories published by Storytellers Ink.
All are fully illustrated.

Black Beauty – the stallion *classic*

Kitty The Raccoon – an abandoned and blind raccoon

If A Seahorse Wore A Saddle - delightful for ages 3-7

The Pacing Mustang – Ernest Thompson Seton's true story

Lobo The Wolf – another gripping true story by Seton

The Lost And Found Puppy – finding a puppy at the shelter

The Living Mountain – the rebirth of Mt. St. Helen's

Father Goose & His Goslings – a dream come true

Sandy Piper – a courageous one-legged bird

William's Story – the adventures of a cat

I Thought I Heard A Tiger Roar – it was really a *meow*

Cousin Charlie, The Crow – a captivating true story

Storytellers Ink
P.O. Box 33398
Seattle, Wa 98133-0398